HIGH SWING

THE COUPLE THAT PLAYS TOGETHER

TENA SELDAN

plicit Press
Erotica Fiction

CHAPTER 1

AS THE PLANE touched down at Charles De Gaulle airport, the rain fell softly, touching the tarmac in perfect synchronicity with the Airbus. Nine hours earlier, before boarding the 7-hour flight to the French Capital, Danni and Stephen were in New York, checking into JFK before they settled into a booth in the first-class waiting lounge, sipping cocktails and speaking in excited whispers about their upcoming honeymoon.

"So, you flying alone," Stephen had asked her suddenly as she sipped one of her last New York cocktails for three weeks.

"My 'husband' is in the bookshop," Danni said, knowing her husband of a year had a very naughty side. He had gone into *game mode*, and she was excited to play along. She already wondered what he had in mind, given where they were, and given that JFK security was almost as tight as she was.

"Are you happy with him?" He was running his fingers up her thigh under the table. Her skirt was long, but this served as no hindrance for a very frisky Stephen.

"He is taking me to Paris..."

"So he's loaded?" Stephen's fingers played on her upper thigh, his eyes looking around the bar to make sure nobody was watching.

"We saved for a year!" Danni put her hand on her husband's, reprimanding him with her eyes. "I'm a married woman!"

"Apparently your not married in an airport bathroom," he said, taking her hand and placing it directly on where he was already hard.

Danni moved her fingers up and down on him, squeezing his thick erection. She seemed to be measuring it with her fingers. Stephen exhaled hard, licked his lips, begged her with his eyes to *unmarry* herself for the next few minutes, and meet him in the bathroom. He put his hand on her thigh again and scanned the room before making contact with her center.

"It's only cheating if we're not in the bathroom," he whispered in her ear, got up, and walked awkwardly to the bathroom. He looked back once, to make sure she would follow.

Of course, she would.

She got to the male bathroom as the door silently swung closed on its hinges. Danni pushed it in quickly, looked around the small bathroom, saw nobody but Stephen slipping into the end stall, followed him, and quietly entered the stall just as three men entered the bathroom.

"Shhh," Stephen motioned, his finger to his mouth as he got down on his knees. He pulled his wife's skirt over his head, found her warm place with his mouth, and devoured it with such care that Danni soon found herself erupting into his mouth.

Stephen stood up, removing his hardness from his track pants and finding the inside of his wife as soon as he came to standing. He pushed her hard against the side of the stall, thrusting quickly in and out of her. The urgency added to the excitement, to the illusion that this moment was stolen and Danni's *husband* might be *returning from the bookstore* any minute.

Danni knew that she wouldn't climax now. Not again at least. It was okay, she really didn't need to. The thrill of this game was enough to keep her satisfied until she could climax at her man's hands later, or in Paris.

"You need to finish up... My husband will be back any minute," she said, sending Stephen into overdrive.

He was now pumping himself furiously into her, pushing her against the fragile wall separating the stalls. He put his hand over her mouth to keep her quiet, ignoring the thuds his thrusts were making.

"Shhh," he said, even though Danni was not the one making the noise.

The bathroom had started to fill, and the four or five men in the room had their eyes on the stall, knowing exactly what was going on. They couldn't ignore it, they didn't want to. All of them stayed at the urinals too long, penises in hand but not peeing. They were all at various stages of arousal, wishing that they were inside the stall.

The thuds became louder before they stopped completely. Stephen had finished, lingering inside Danni for a minute, to allow himself the time to recover. When he did, he pulled himself from her, slowly, and then kissed the side of her neck. He let her skirt fall back over her legs but quickly put his hand underneath it, pulling up his pants with the other hand.

He found the inside of her with his fingers and connected his mouth to hers. Both of them could hear the movement outside the stall and so they knew they couldn't move, not yet. So Stephen used the time to bring Danni to a controlled climax, silencing her with his mouth on hers, his tongue deep in her face.

His long fingers moved easily inside her, mixing his own juice with her natural moisture. He went deep, pulling Danni closer and closer to an orgasm she didn't think she would have. She started to exhale into his mouth and Stephen kissed her harder, pushing his finger just a little deeper.

"We're gonna miss the flight," she said, pressing her sweaty face against the door.

"No, we're not!" Stephen reassured her, slowly opening the door as Danni pulled herself together.

He was hard again, but there really was nothing he could do about this right now. He exited the stall, washed his hands just because, and nodded to the two men left at the urinals. They both came over to him and also washed their hands, giving the stall the side-eye. Danni was trapped inside, the door half-open.

Then they winked at Stephen and left, giving Danni a short window to exit. She did, going into the female bathroom next door to wash her face and fix her hair. Then she met Stephen at the booth where they had time for one more drink before they heard their boarding call.

Seven hours later they arrived to a rainy Paris morning, both of them a little tired but incredibly excited!

CHAPTER 2

THE INTERCONTINENTAL WAS A BEAUTIFUL HOTEL. It was the perfect blend of simple and sophisticated. Their room was on the second floor, with a grand view of the street below. Paris was certainly living up to all their expectations.

"We should have learned a little bit of French, don't you think," Danni said, turning on the faucets before she pulled her skirt off, needing to shower. Stephan was already naked behind her in the bathroom, also needing a shower before he had a post-flight nap.

"We'll get by, I'm sure," he said, wrapping a towel around his waist to attend to an unexpected knock on the door.

He re-entered the bathroom, flutes in hand. "Compliments of the hotel," he said, touching his glass gently to his wife's before kissing her on her forehead, resurrecting his erection.

"Already, soldier?" she asked, looking down at him with a smile on her face.

"You do this to me!"

She really did. Stephen never enjoyed lovemaking as much as he did with Danni. They just fit together, body and mind. Even when he started introducing his *'games,'* she let her discomfort and initial apprehension take a backseat, quickly. She played along immediately, and soon enough, more and more in the year and a half since they started playing, she found that she liked them and that they excited her immensely.

They put their glasses down on the counter and got under the warm shower. They weren't tired, but they knew that they needed to take it easy today, for a few hours at least. The next three weeks were loosely structured, and they had no commitments. But there was so much to do in and around Paris that they wanted to be as energized as possible.

It had taken them the best part of the year to save for this honeymoon, deciding first to purchase a home, his and hers Mercedes', and get their careers established. Stephen and Danni were both junior partners at different law firms, quite an achievement for two people in their late 20s, so they were not broke. They just had their priorities straight!

The water fell over them like the rain outside, the jet pressure in the showerhead perfect. Stephen half-washed half-massaged Danni's back, enjoying the feeling of her beautiful skin on his fingers. He moved his hands over all of her, her own fingers moving up and down on his hardness.

They were not trying to be intimate. They just were. If this playful fondling led to an orgasm, so be it. If it didn't, that was okay too. They just enjoyed touching each other, and so they did for as long as they were under the shower.

Danni fell asleep first, naked under the covers. It wasn't cold, but Stephen had put the air-conditioner on so she just needed something over her. He lay beside her, on top of the covers, checking Paris out online on his cellphone with one hand, the other moving through Danni's hair.

She enjoyed sleeping like this.

Stephen made a dinner reservation for them and arranged a cooking class for the weekend. He also arranged for them to meet with an estate agent just so that they could have a look at some apartments in the city. He had no intention to purchase, though; he just really liked viewing property.

About an hour later, he was also asleep!

When Danni woke up, she was alone. A note beside the bed let her know that they had a 6:30 dinner reservation and that Stephen would be back shortly. She wondered, as she started to unpack their suitcases, where he was, and more specifically, what he was up to.

The thought, the many possibilities, excited her, and she poured herself some more champagne, enjoying the taste of the *good stuff*, and continued her unpacking, which really was just her choosing outfits for Stephen and herself to wear to dinner.

"Hello Husband,' she said as Stephen walked in.

"Hello Wifey," he said, pulling her close to him, pleased to find her still naked. He pulled his shorts down, kicked off his sneakers, and let her pull off his t-shirt. Then he reached for her glass and finished the champagne, kissing her passionately as his eyes went to the clothing on the sofa.

"And?"

"Dinner!"

"Right..."

"So, where were you?" she asked, as he lifted her off the floor and held her tightly against himself.

"Just checking out the hotel," he said, before laying her on the bed, getting on his knees, and sinking his face between her legs.

She started to speak, but couldn't suddenly, his tongue moving inside her already. She loved everything he did to her, but this was certainly one of her favorites. He had a way of moving in her with just his tongue that was interesting and that felt incredibly new every time. She never knew what to expect, and every time she was pleasantly surprised.

Danni wondered, between focusing on trying to breathe and her body literally giving itself to Stephen if he planned each of these particular encounters. There were things that he did with his face in her hidden space that were unpredictable, unexpected. But then there were things about it that felt perfectly choreographed.

She suddenly wasn't thinking about where Stephen had been. Her body had overtaken her senses and stripped her of all sensibilities. If she tried to string a coherent sentence together, she knew it would be impossible. Her everything now belonged to him, which she knew, but this moment, now, reminded her that he was determined that she never forgot it.

Stephen held her thighs tightly, pressing her legs into the bed as he dug deeper into her with his tongue. She lifted her back completely off the bed as she exploded hard into his mouth, every part of her body on fire.

He left her to recover as he showered and got ready for dinner. She showered about fifteen minutes later, and they left the room with incredibly satisfied looks about the both of them.

CHAPTER 3

DINNER WAS GOOD. It was cozy and intimate, and the food was delicious. They finished the last of the second bottle of wine, and were drinking coffee now, and eating a variety of chocolate-covered fruit slices. Feeding each other the fruit was cute, and certainly not out of place, a couple full-on making out a few tables away.

"I've arranged for us to view apartments tomorrow if that's okay!" Stephen said, putting the last piece of fruit in his own mouth.

"Of course it is. Who with?" She was already planning a game of her own in her head, the apartment viewing offering her an interesting twist.

"Paul Du Bois, I'll send you a link!" Stephen sent the link before he'd finished the sentence!

Danni pulled Stephen to her and nibbled on his ear. Her lips smelled of strong coffee, and when Stephen kissed her, she tasted like coffee and dark chocolate. This was enough to set him off again, and he put her hand on him so that she could feel the consequences of what she was doing to him.

"You're joking," she smiled.

"Does this feel like a joke to you?" he asked, standing up only after he had positioned himself as inconspicuously as possible in his pants. He put her scarf over her shoulders, and they left the restaurant, walking into the Paris night, thankful that it had stopped raining so that they could walk the few blocks to the hotel.

Love seemed to be everywhere. Couples were huddled in the shadows all around them. Around fountains, under street lights, in the doorways to buildings, Paris seemed to be putting on its best performance for them.

"It's beautiful here..." Danni said.

"You're beautiful!" Stephen whispered, finding a spot against the side of a building just dark enough for them to disappear.

He cupped his wife's face in his hands, tenderly. As tenderly, he brought his mouth to hers, planting what felt like a hundred kisses on her lips, each one perfect and complete. He pushed himself up against her, pulling her into him at the same time. Then their mouths met again, and their tongues danced together in the darkness.

There were no games now. There was just pure, genuine love between two people who had grown even more in love with one another in the year since they were married. They kissed long, deep. They looked deep into each other's eyes and said everything they wanted to, with no words.

Back at the hotel too, the playfulness had ceased. There were no roles, no characters. There was just a husband making deep and passionate love with and to his wife. And make love they did.

When eventually they fell asleep, they were well and truly spent. The beautiful tangled mess that was their bodies lay sprawled at a diagonal across the bed. Danni and Stephen were that tantalizing kind of tired they knew would see them fresh and ready the following day.

———

The GPS location of the first apartment saw them standing outside a beautiful building on the Champs-Elysees. The architecture was grand, and Stephen especially couldn't wait to get up to the 2-bedroom apartment on the seventh floor. Danni was enjoying the beauty of the setting, and the slightly overcast morning.

"Stephen?" A French accent said, somewhere behind them. They both turned to find the most stylish couple they had ever seen walking toward them. "This is my wife, Sophia, and this is..." Paul was looking at Danni in a way that, were they not in Paris, would have been quite inappropriate.

"This beautiful young thing is my wife, Danni!"

The two men pulled the other's wife to them and kissed them on each cheek. Stephen couldn't help but linger on Sophia for a minute. She smelled wonderfully of *watermelon*. The scent was light, fresh. It was her perfume, he knew, and made a mental note to ask her what it was later. He could already imagine this fusion of fruit and spice on Danni, the thought arousing him just a little.

Danni let Paul breathe her in, too. He held her in a way that let her know he was enjoying it. Danni felt diminutive in his grip, the almost too-tall Frenchman half-lifting her off the stone road, his large hands on her hips, and then on her shoulders making her feel almost vulnerable to this giant with a beautiful smile.

The apartment was exquisite. Stephen would have put

in an offer to purchase on the spot, had he discussed it with Danni first. The other two they viewed were equally magnificent. They were small, yes, but their functional layout made this easy to overlook. Stephen really was in awe.

"So, now that we've gotten the business end of things sorted, can we buy you a drink?" Paul was being polite, Stephen thought, and he knew that if they turned him down, this might be seen as offensive.

"Sounds great," he said, looking at Danni for confirmation.

Sophia took Danni by the hand and they walked out in front, Sophia wanting to know everything they had planned for their honeymoon. Paul and Stephen kept an acceptable following distance, discussing the intricate complexities of purchasing property in Paris!

" We must have dinner one night before you leave. I'd love for you to see our apartment. It's not for sale, but it really gives you a great idea of what is possible!" Paul said this, his eyes on Danni even though he was essentially talking to Stephen.

"We'd love that," Danni said, trying to downplay the fact that he was staring at her, responding to give his gaze purpose.

"That's settled then. You'll let us know," Sophia said, bringing herself close to Stephen again, letting him get one final whiff of her watermelon mist!

They parted ways in the busy *market district,* Stephen and Danni wanting to absorb themselves in French culture and process the very strange vibe of this mid-day drink. It was pleasant, for the most part, but there seemed to be an undertow that neither Danni nor Stephen could quite put their finger on!

CHAPTER 4

"THAT WAS VERY STRANGE, wasn't it?" Danni said as she blow-dried her hair in the bathroom.

"I think it's just the way they are, you know, the French!"

"I don't think so... Are we going to go?"

"Don't you want to?" Stephen was standing in the bathroom now.

"I don't know..."

The phone rang. Stephen needed to pee, so Danni got it. When she hung up she came into the bathroom. "That was weird. Apparently, there's a package for me at reception."

"For you? Or us?" Stephen put himself away and washed his hands. He was watching Danni through the mirror pulling on shorts.

"Me, that's what they said. I'll be right back, okay. Then we can decide what we're doing for dinner!"

Danni walked out of the room still tying her hair into a ponytail. She walked quickly towards the stairs, springing down them, curious about what the package might be. Nobody from the office had called her, so it couldn't be work. She could think of nothing else though, assuming that the package arrived before the call. Going through legal documents was not how she thought she'd be enjoying her honeymoon, she thought, as she walked up to the receptionist.

The receptionist smiled, handing her a small envelope. "Is this it?" she asked.

"Yes, madam, this is all!"

She opened the envelope as she walked up the stairs. The card inside it said, simply, ***307 and a half!*** She was standing outside their room door when it finally clicked. This was another game, and her next clue was going to be found on the third floor.

As Danni walked towards room 307, she did wonder what the *half* was, and then she saw it. At the end of the hall, right between rooms 307 and 308 was an unmarked door. She tried the handle, and the door opened easily. Danni pulled it open slowly, looking into the darkness, almost expecting to see Stephen there.

When her eyes had adjusted, she spotted another envelope. She opened it in the light of the hallway, and read the instructions:

Leave your panties in the closet, and make your way up on to the roof!

Danni looked down the hall, waited for a couple to enter their room just a few doors from where she was, and then slipped into the tight space. She fitted, but only just. Standing straight, she struggled to get her shorts, and then her panties, off. When she stepped back out into the hall, she was genuinely flushed.

Walking up the stairs to the roof, Danni wondered what the view must be like from atop The Intercontinental. She was wondering a lot of other things really, but she knew better than to build up any sort of expectation in her mind. She knew she would be surprised, and it was this element that excited her.

It was this new excitement that brought outsides of her that she hadn't even known existed. She learned that she had, before Stephen, been rather suppressed. This new version of herself was liberated, and she loved it!

She couldn't find the roof suddenly, having walked up and down the last flight of stairs a number of times. Danni was really tired now, but still really excited. She walked down the hall to the opposite side, pushing what looked like a service door. The stairs led upwards, Danni stepping quickly now, thinking that she had kept Stephen waiting a little too long.

When she finally stepped out onto the roof, the freshness of the night brushed across her face. It wasn't cold, but she did feel a bit of a nip. She walked straight to the edge of the roof and looked over, taking in the breathtaking view.

"You've been very, very naughty, li'l miss!" Stephen's voice was husky and low.

Danni wanted to turn around, but his hands kept her against the railing, stopping her from looking at him. Then he held her panties out in front of her, and whispered in her ear, "do you make a habit of leaving your underwear in utility closets?"

"I was getting hot," she mumbled.

"Hot?" he said, unbuttoning her shorts and sending a hand down her front. He found her incredibly *hot*!

Stephen put the panties in his mouth and pulled her shorts down and off. He bent her over the railings and moved the lace in his mouth over the back of her legs. Then he ran this tiny garment along with his lips over her lips, holding her legs apart. She shivered her back straightening, only to be pushed back down as Stephen stood up behind her again.

"Bad things happen to bad, bad wo..." he started to say.

"I've been very, very bad!" she interrupted.

"Yes, yes you have," he whispered, wetting her other hole with her own moisture from her front.

He went into this incredibly tight space, slowly and with just one finger. This digit moved in all the way, very slowly, with great care despite his own excitement. Then the finger was moving out of her, all the way, before collecting more moisture from her and sending the finger back in.

She couldn't think, as the finger was suddenly replaced by his own head. He wanted inside her now, and she wanted him there. As her body gave way, first to his head and then to every inch of him, she gripped the railing and moved back on him, giving him full permission to do whatever he wanted as punishment for her *bad*.

He did!

CHAPTER 5

"THAT WAS A GREAT COOKING CLASS," Danni said, Stephen, looking at his mobile phone. He turned the phone so that she could read it. It was an email from the *Du Bois*, wondering if they'd had time to think about their invitation.

"Let's go..." he said, not quite asking her.

"Let's," she said, knowing that he probably really wanted to go, for whatever reason. She thought of her own game, the one she was planning when she'd heard they would be looking at apartments. Wondering if she might be able to play it at the dinner party, she packed her own set of envelopes in her purse, out of view of Stephen, before they went down to the car that had been sent for them.

The apartment was near the Eiffel Tower, or rather, it had a spectacular view of this iconic structure from its wrap-around balcony. The penthouse was large, split into four levels even though it just had two bedrooms. It was grand in every respect, and perfect, Danni thought, for her game.

She knew she didn't have her husband's skills as a

gamemaster, but she knew that where she lacked in creativity, the setting of the game would make up for it. As Sophia showed her around the space, the men sampling Paul's whiskey collection, she felt Sophia's eyes on her. Still, she managed to place, strategically, the clues she had written, hoping that they would work.

"You really have a lovely home," she said to Paul when she and Sophia stepped out onto the balcony.

"Thank you," Paul said, pulling her to him and kissing the side of her face. She looked at Stephen, a question mark on her face. Stephen threw her his 'hes French' look, and smiled at her discomfort. He really didn't think too much of it, not sure if it actually was, but assuming that this over-display of affection was cultural.

Sophia took Stephen into the kitchen, wanting him to taste her *coq au vin*, or rather the sauce, just before she served it. Paul needed the bathroom, leaving Danni alone on the balcony. She took the time to text her husband clue number one, which should, she hoped, get their game going.

She needed something to distract her from the incredible distraction that was Paul!

Stephen looked at his phone as it vibrated in his hand. ***The second floor, bathroom***, is all the message said. He looked at Danni out on the balcony. She wasn't looking at him. He tasted the sauce and excused himself. He went up to the second floor, meeting Paul as he exited the bathroom.

"I'm sorry, I should have told you there was a bathroom downstairs," he said, an envelope in his hand.

"This is obviously the preferred one," Stephen said.

"I do like it!"

Paul walked down the stairs, reading the clue in the envelope that wasn't meant for him.

"Let tonight be interesting... How interesting depends on where you find my panties..."

Paul walked to his wife and showed her the note. She smiled as both of them looked out onto the balcony at Danni, who was now looking at them. She felt uncomfortable, raising her glass to them. The French couple returned this gesture, the smiles on their faces growing.

Stephen came back downstairs, and the three of them joined Danni outside. He shrugged his shoulders, a *'whats up'* look on his face. Danni was confused as Sophia took her over to the plush balcony sofa, and sat them down side by side. Paul poured another drink for himself and Stephen, pointing at the woman with his glass so that Stephen was now looking at the two beauties perched on the couch.

Suddenly, Sophia reached under her skirt, in full view of everyone, and pulled her own panties down. "Now we're both not wearing any underwear," she whispered loudly to Danni.

"Say what now?" Danni asked, looking at Stephen, the look on her face saying *'I told you so!'*

His own eyes moved from Danni to Sophia, who was now walking toward her husband. She pulled him down and kissed him on his mouth as she guided his fingers between her legs. She seemed to mount his hand, taking at least one of his fingers into herself!"

"I said...to Paul...as soon as we met...that you...would...be open...to it!" She was speaking in an almost stutter, the single sentence broken by her up-down movement on his finger.

Danni and Stephen were speechless. They were both suddenly very aroused, but no words were coming out of their mouths. It seemed, suddenly, like they were too far from each other, and so Stephen made the move to the couch.

Paul lifted his wife effortlessly off the floor, and she wrapped her legs around his waist, his finger still snug between her legs. Their lips were still locked too, so no clarification was coming any time soon. All Danni and Stephen could do was watch and wait.

Sophia was moving up and down, and then around and around, taking Paul's thick digit completely into her with every movement. Then she pulled her mouth from her husband's, looked back at the two people looking at them in disbelief, and dismounted, the grace of a gymnast.

She walked over to Danni and whispered in her ear, "he found your note!"

She wanted to explain, Stephen pulling on her hand, silencing her. She wondered what this meant, and excused herself. Stephen followed her to the kitchen, and then into the downstairs bathroom.

"That note was meant for you..." she said.

" I didn't see it!"

" I know, he did. And now they think we're *open to it!*"

There was a moment of protracted silence. And then, very slowly, Stephen asked, *"are we?"*

CHAPTER 6

STEPHEN WALKED OUT BEHIND DANNI, kissing her on the back of her neck. They made their way to the opposite end of the sofa, the other end occupied by Paul and Sophia. Paul's shirt was off, and Sophia's skirt was lifted high above her waist. His finger was still moving gently in and out of her, their mouths still locked.

Danni straddled her husband's lap, kissing his face as Stephen unbuttoned his own shirt. Then her mouth was moving over his chest as his fingers found her thighs under her skirt. He moved her up and down on himself, pushing her hard against the zip of his trousers.

Her face was gently moved off his chest, her head tilted back. Without warning Paul's lips found hers, and he was kissing her like only the French can. Despite herself, she was quickly kissing him back. Sophia's mouth found Stephen's before he could protest, and he was silenced by the scent of watermelon.

Paul lifted Danni from her husband, his own wife taking her place. His fingers expertly freed Danni of her skirt, his teeth and tongue unbuttoning her shirt, all without putting her down. He unbuttoned his jeans and pulled his zip down, just to give his erection breathing room. He made no move to pull his jeans down, though, kissing Danni again instead.

Danni had her eyes on Stephen, who despite a now naked Sophia working on his jeans button, was also looking at her. This wasn't how they thought this evening would go, but now they were definitely in it. With their eyes, they gave each other permission, allowing themselves this experience.

Stephen took Sophia's near-perfect nipples in his mouth. She arched, rubbing her wet pink against his now exposed hard place. She pulled his hair, bringing herself harder against him. The fusion of their juices made the glide an incredibly smooth ride. Sophia had such control of her body, that even though Stephen was already thinking of her *inside*, he knew that he wouldn't get there until she let him.

Stephen also wanted Danni to take the plunge first, too, just in case this was a problem later. And by the looks of things, Paul pulling his jeans down with one hand, still holding Danni up with the other, he suspected that he wouldn't have to wait too long. So he just relaxed into the sofa, letting Sophia do what she wanted.

She slithered off his lap, and pulled his jeans off completely, leaving his underwear around his knees. Then she came up, and kissed his pelvic bone, running her nose against his pubic hair as she moved from one side of his shaft to the other.

Then she was running the tip of her tongue on his head, Stephen watching her now. He gripped the base of himself, held and pointed his manhood so that she could work on it easily. Danni's legs were wrapped around Paul's neck, his tongue working the exterior of her almost as expertly as Stephen did. Stephen didn't want to see how his wife was enjoying this, even though they too were back on the sofa. He chose his moment and thrust into Sophia's mouth, to distract himself from Danni's sensual moaning.

Sophia swallowed him fast, letting him thrust into her mouth a few times before squeezing his meat tightly with her lips. Then she started moving up and down on him, at a slower pace than his thrusting, but as delicious. He looked over at Danni briefly, her back arched, her eyes closed. Paul's tongue had found the tightness of her *inside*, and she was thoroughly enjoying it.

Stephen was of course also enjoying Sophia's mouth on him, but he'd be lying if he didn't admit to himself that he was a little bit jealous. He started to question if this was a good idea, and then remembered that he had said, not in so many words, that it was. So he really couldn't be the one who brought the evening to an end and stormed off with his wife.

Instead, he lifted Sophia off him and pulled her up so that he was tasting himself in her mouth. Then he lifted Sophia so that she was standing on the sofa, her legs on either side of him, her *lady parts* front and center, square with his face. He gripped her firm behind, and gently pushed his face into her. Anything Paul could do, he could do. And he was determined to do it better.

He breathed her into him before teasing her with his tongue. Then he was kissing her with his lips, and then with his lips and tongue. When he started nibbling on her carefully with his teeth she almost fell back, saved by his hold on her rear. Then he was licking again, carefully lapping up the drizzle emanating from her.

When he was nibbling again, just a little harder, she moaned, loudly. He moved his tongue over the places he had just bitten before biting a bit harder. She moaned louder still, and so again he licked, and bit. He was proud of himself for finding one of her spots so quickly, much to his surprise, since he hadn't explored or experienced another woman since he met Danni.

When his tongue finally moved into her she held on to his head, needing to steady herself. She tasted like she smelled, and this excited Stephen even more. He sent his tongue as deep into her as it would go, and let it settle and sit, soaking up her delicious odor.

Sophia moved herself on his tongue, slowly so as not to evict it. She seemed to love this invasion, pulling on his hair hard with each small movement of her middle. Again Stephen moved just his eyes to where Danni's legs were now in the air, Paul's hands around her ankles. She was looking at Paul now, who was licking her lips hard. His eyes were locked with hers as he moved his tongue against the entire surface exterior of her *near erupting* volcano.

She wanted his tongue back inside her, but Paul seemed to be focused on just the outside. It felt incredible, but it also created a longing inside her that made this experience terribly frustrating. But then, with absolutely no warning, she was flowing, audibly, into his mouth and all over his face. Danni screamed, loudly, despite herself, and in spite of her husband who was watching her closely in disbelief.

Stephen returned his focus to Sophia, who was also now watching Danni and Paul, wanting to see what the source of Stephen's distraction was. He pushed her away from his face and laid her down on the sofa. Connecting again with her *pleasure palace*, he didn't lick but again went all the way in with his tongue. He pulled all the way out quickly, before going in again, slower.

Then pace was steady, his rhythm consistent. He could have rushed it, he knew, brought her to a swift orgasm. Instead, he opted for slow and steady, and the completeness of her climax let him know that it was the right move!

CHAPTER 7

SOPHIA AND DANNI looked at each other, Paul and Stephen also sharing a stare. Nobody spoke, and it was clear that the night could go one of two ways, now that the women had climaxed, rather spectacularly.

The moment was extremely tense, Danni and Stephen never having done this before, Sophia and Paul thinking that they had. So it seemed like they would miss a great opportunity, if they didn't come clean, because neither Stephen nor Danni knew what to do now, and it seemed the other couple had placed the ball in their court.

"Well done," Stephen said to Paul, his eyes on Danni.

"Pleasing her was my pleasure," he said, also looking at Danni as he went to get drinks.

Sophia was running her fingers up and down on Stephen's hardness, the fingers of her other hand teasing Danni's nipples. Paul arrived back, put the tray down, and towered over Danni, bending to kiss her and then his wife in tandem.

Then Sophia was kissing Stephen, deeply. Her scent really sent him into another world completely, because he lifted her off the sofa and laid her on her back closer to him. He caught a glimpse of Paul sitting down in the space Sophia had just occupied. Then all his attention was on Sophia as he brought himself down on top of her, kissing her neck, rubbing the length of himself against her.

She parted her legs and he pressed down harder. Thoughts of Danni snuck into his head and he lifted himself off Sophia slightly. He wanted to scream, wafts of watermelon around his head, inside it. He couldn't resist much longer, and he was again rubbing himself against her. He really wanted to be inside Sophia, just once, just briefly. But he couldn't turn around now to see what was happening behind him, so he wasn't sure.

Danni was on top of Paul. They were also kissing, their *yearning parts* rubbing against each other. He was equally mesmerized by Danni, more so perhaps. And if his massive hard-on was to be believed, he also wanted nothing more than to be inside her, fast. Danni and Sophia were similar in size and weight, so Paul definitely had a type. The differences between him and Stephen, however, were striking, and Paul wasn't sure if big and *BIG* were Danni's type.

She hadn't thought of her type in a while. When she had met and married Stephen, he was her type. He still was, actually. But this extra-large Frenchman presented her with a unique opportunity to test her limits. And she was open to being tested, her husband looking eager to test his own abilities.

Danni wanted to tell him that it was okay, sensing somehow his apprehension. She couldn't, though, because he wasn't looking at her. He couldn't look at her without removing himself completely from Sophia. Danni would have to think of a creative way to let him know that he had the green light.

She positioned herself on Paul, not quite ready yet but knowing that her husband would let himself go once he was sure that she had. Paul was huge, and she couldn't breathe as he inched inside her. She moaned loudly, almost too loudly. She worked herself down on him until she could go no deeper.

Paul was looking directly into her eyes. She was looking directly at him, moving up now, before easing herself back down. She couldn't breathe again, and so any sounds were impossible. She needed to get comfortable with this mass inside her first she knew before she could think of signaling her husband with sound.

She breathed out as she lifted herself up the shaft, breathing in as she went back down on it. Still deathly silent, she repeated this over and over again, very very slowly. Then she flipped it, breathing in on the up, and out on the down. It made no difference, the size of the man inside her still bordering on unbearable.

Her moisture didn't do much to help her out. She was streaming now, flowing like a brook from her pleasure center, but Paul really was big, and it was taking her a minute to adjust. Stephen had a decent size on him, too, but it wasn't Paul. And also, she was used to her husband, who seemed to have an intimate understanding of her body. The man inside her now was a relative stranger, and so her body was putting up a bit of a fight.

Paul put his hands on her waist. He held her to himself so that she could no longer move. Then he started to thrust into her and then out. In and out, slowly in then slowly out. He needed her to stop being in control now. He needed her to relax and let go, to let him in and do what he knew he could do.

Now Danni was moaning. She was screaming in joyous

ecstasy as Paul sent himself all the way inside her. She wasn't giving away just yet, and it seemed that she wouldn't. But Paul had arrested full control of the situation now, and he was pulling all the right sounds from Danni.

He absolutely loved it!

She was breathing easier now, deeper. Her moans were gorgeous murmurs, and these sounds were definitely letting Stephen know exactly what was going on behind them now. He was still just rubbing himself against Sophia, albeit harder. He knew that it was game on now, and he just needed to get exactly what the game plan was, right in his head.

Stephen was nervous suddenly. He was listening to his wife, listening to Paul's grunts. He wanted to make sure that he delivered on Sophia because if he didn't, he knew he'd be disappointed in himself. He also didn't want Sophia to feel like she got the short end of the stick, *his stick already shorter* anyway.

He took a deep breath, and started to make his own entry into the beautiful women underneath him who still smelled like freshly cut watermelon!

CHAPTER 8

AS STEPHEN SUNK INTO SOPHIA, the balcony seemed to melt away underneath them and around him. He could still hear Danni and Paul, but this had become the background music to his own pleasure. Selfish and Stephen were not two words that usually went together, but as he made his way deeper into Sophia, it really was all about him. He could think of nothing else.

He had his eyes closed. He had gotten all the way inside her, not thrusting yet, not moving. He was just enjoying the sensation of being in her, all the way, and the smell coming up off her was *inspiring*. It made him want to do things with her and to her, things that he wasn't sure he was capable of doing, having never done them before. Perhaps it was just the newness of it all, perhaps the watermelon. Whatever it was, he was certainly not himself.

When he did start to move, out and then in, all the way out and then all the way in, his focus started to return. His senses were heightened and he could feel and smell everything. He could also hear everything, which meant that the sounds behind him were no longer just background. Fortunately, the sounds coming from Sophia were not back-grounded either.

His legs straightened, and he sunk into her deeper. At least that's how it felt. Then he sort of bent his legs, lifting Sophia's too, and he had control of his delivery. His delivery was meticulous, and on each full inward thrust, Sophia stuttered something in French.

"Perhaps we should have gotten those lessons after all," he said, loudly but to himself.

Sophia's eyes were also closed. She had spread her legs so far now that Stephen could only take a hold of her thighs. He was thrusting into her just that much harder now, and she was loving every single thrust. There was absolutely no barrier to entry, and Stephen and Sophia were making the most of this uninhibited connection.

She started to pant, and Stephen opened his eyes to look at her. Surely he couldn't have brought her *there* quite yet? It was too soon, for him at least. Danni and Paul were still magically connected themselves, but from the sounds emanating from them, they were nowhere near anything even vaguely resembling climax.

Stephen couldn't focus on what was happening behind him. He needed to focus on Sophia, needed to stay her orgasm. She was panting louder, his thrusts harder. He needed to stop moving, but he knew that arresting her bliss might anger the European woman whose temperament he wasn't fully aware of, yet.

He put his mouth on hers, and pulled himself almost completely from her, slowing down his movement. Then he went back inside her, as slowly, hoping that the fact that he was at least still thrusting made up for his change in pace. He knew he had to go slower if he was going to stop her explosion, and it worked. Her eyes were opened too now, and she was looking at him trying to figure out what his plan was.

She wrapped her legs around him, pulling him into herself. He was careful not to play into her hands, not to give in to the urge to go at it hard and fast. It really took everything in him, because bringing her to climax would be a notch on his belt. Then he thought of Paul steadily bringing his own wife closer and closer and he realized that Sophia knew pleasure.

Stephen rolled so that his back was against the back of the sofa. Sophia moved her leg from underneath him and watched as Stephen moved in and out of her slower now. Side by side, facing one another, they both watched their connection, the visuals feeding both their arousal.

He was harder, and he felt that he might accidentally spill over into her. Sophia seemed wetter, somehow, and he wondered if she hadn't perhaps already reached her end. He listened, closely, more to her than to the two whose sounds had also picked up speed. Hoping he was reading her right, Stephen maintained his pace, hoping that there wouldn't be too much of a gap between her climax and his own.

Danni was tumbling into her own orgasm now. Paul just held on to her tightly, moving her up and down, not quite quickly, not quite not. Giving him control was easy because he took it without asking. But when he was in full control, he knew exactly what to do with it, and what to do with her.

Paul was a master at all things carnal, and this mastery carried easily even to his climax. He wasn't overly excited, moving Danni on him with the same rhythm that brought her to her own end. He kept a steady grip on her even as he was spilling himself into her, quite excessively. At the last minute, he let her go and let her bring them down from the cloud he had managed to get them on.

Stephen was moving faster now, his own end in sight. He was still not sure of Sophia's state, but when it was her moving them so that he was now on his back, he knew. She hadn't yet erupted, but she really wanted to. And she was not going to allow him to keep her back from it any longer.

He watched her move eagerly on him. She pulled him in every direction, using her body in ways he had never thought possible. Stephen hoped that Danni was watching so that she might try this on him later. He made notes on some of the things that Paul had done so far, for the same reason.

"Are you ready," she asked him, really asking herself because she had taken charge now. She ground herself against him harder and harder, bringing herself so close that it was she who was now being selfish. Stephen was reduced to a means to an end, and her end was spectacular.

Stephen's end was equally spectacular!

CHAPTER 9

STEPHEN AND PAUL reclaimed their wives. They relaxed into the sofa, holding on to their women, drinking and chatting casually. They didn't speak about what had just happened, what was still happening. It seemed to be the accepted state of current affairs, and they were all pleased with this no holds barred access to each other's spouses.

"Is anybody hungry?" Sophia was touching herself and her husband, looking at Danni who still seemed stuck in her haze.

"No, I'm good," Danni said, looking right back at Sophia, who seemed to want to ask her something.

"He's incredible..." Sophia said, not quite a question.

"Yes, he is," Danni said, not quite an answer.

Paul and Stephen looked at each other and gave each other a gentlemen's nod. They also declined the offer of food, helping themselves to some snacks on a platter that had been sitting on the balcony unattended since they arrived instead. It was really an evening filled with lessons and lust, the students and the teachers equally confident.

Sophia was looking at Danni again, and Danni wasn't sure what to do with herself. She turned to Stephen and took a cracker from him, licking his fingers as they stayed in her mouth. She turned her body to face him too now, Sophia's piercing stare getting uncomfortable. Danni wondered, as she leaned over into Stephen, if her performance with Paul earlier somehow offended her.

How could it, though? Sophia had just had what sounded like an epic experience with Stephen, and this really didn't bother her. She did find it strange how unbothered she was by this, especially given that this was really their first time. Danni knew though that this offense didn't exist. It couldn't, because Paul and Sophia had extensive experience in this *experience*!

Stephen was kissing Danni, in that familiar way that she knew and liked. She was on her knees on the sofa, pressing her face into Stephen's, their tongues engaged in a conversation with no words. Sophia looked at her husband, then she looked at Danni again. There was something on her mind, something she wanted badly to do, but she wasn't sure how she was going to make her move.

And then she did!

Sophia moved to Danni and parted her legs. She slithered underneath them so that she was now face to face with the part of Stephen that was just inside her. She kissed it, and then she took him into her mouth, getting him hard rather quickly. Danni looked down to where her husband was again in a part of Sophia. She wanted her to move so that she could taste her husband. But Sophia seemed to have a hold.

Suddenly Sophia was off him, moving to give Danni access. She had to move down slightly to reach him, but when she did, she took him into her mouth, slowly. Sophia had moved as Danni moved, Paul watching his own wife closely. He knew what she wanted to do, and he knew that she was going to try, any minute now, so he moved closer just a bit, to get a better view.

Underneath Danni, Sophia turned onto her back, Danni hanging over her. She lifted her head and made contact with her, and Danni stopped moving on her husband. She looked down between her legs and was surprised at what she saw. Sophia was nibbling, eyes closed, on her. She was eating her out like a meal, and this feeling, the sensation of it, was confusing.

It felt good, but just what good was in this new situation she was not sure. She knew it felt interesting and strange, but again strange and interesting lost their meaning. Stephen was also watching this, wanting Danni's mouth on him again because the sight of a woman on his woman was thrilling. Paul was as thrilled, running his fingers over Danni's behind, parting her cheeks and tapping ever so lightly with his thick index directly on her *rosebud*.

Danni was still trying to make sense of the sensations between her legs when her husband gently motioned her head back onto himself. He wanted her to relax into it, needed her to relax into it because this was an experience Stephen really felt she needed to have. It was an experience *he* needed to have.

Paul was watching Stephen now, a sly smile on his face. He held on to Danni's derriere with just one hand, the other hand going down between Sophia's legs. Then he was going in, into his wife's wet front, and slowly into Danni's back. He was dripping from his own erection, but there was nobody to attend to him. He watched instead as Stephen's erection was being swiftly attended to by his wife's all too perfect mouth!

Stephen lowered himself to the couch, getting more comfortable. Danni held herself up by placing her palms on his legs while her mouth moved up and down. Sophia was moaning loudly now as she sent her tongue into Danni in short movements. Then she was kissing her like she had kissed her husband, pulling the sweetest nectar from between Danni's thighs.

Paul's finger went deep into Danni and she tensed. As it moved around, she relaxed more and more, and the movement of this finger was easier. Then another finger was added, and again Danni tensed. Paul was in no hurry, so he just settled these two fingers in her, not moving them. He added a second finger to Sophia, but these fingers moved aggressively in and out of her.

He knew how she liked to be touched. He was aware of her body and he responded accordingly. Sophia hung onto Danni now, her hands around her lower back as she continued to devour her. Danni was caught in a multi-way pleasure circuit that she was scared might electrocute her now.

She tried to focus on Stephen but couldn't. She was trying to pick a pleasure to focus on, but couldn't decide. His *tush* was being invaded, but not assaulted. Her front was being assaulted but not invaded. She really had no idea what was happening to her but he definitely did not want it to stop!

CHAPTER 10

PAUL PULLED his fingers from her. He parted her cheeks, having also removed his fingers from his wife. Then he connected with her bud, and it bloomed, coming to an incredible life. His tongue moved over her, Sophia's tongue working deliciously on her lips. Again she wasn't sure what was going on, but she liked it, a lot.

Then Paul's tongue was inside her, and it felt incredible. She was tight. But his tongue was incredibly powerful. So the entry was easy, but just because Paul was very good at what he was doing.

Stephen watched Paul, wondering why he had never gone into this particular hole with such verve. He had explored her there before, but not with the eagerness he was witnessing right now. He always handled it with such care, but he always thought that this was the way Danni liked it.

When Paul lifted his mouth from Danni, and looked at Stephen, he was throwing him a look that said he appreciated the lesson. Stephen had already lined up, in his head, a series of games that would make his and his wife's intimate life more memorable than it had been so far.

He nodded at Paul, giving him permission to do whatever he wanted. He knew now, that he would have full access to Danni for the rest of their lives.

Paul pointed himself towards Danni's entrance and slid into her quickly. His hardness made this entry easy, and the delicious squeeze of the space made him start to thrust immediately. He reached for Sophia, found her wetness with two fingers, and as he fed himself to Danni, he worked with the same skill, using just his fingers, on his own wife!

Stephen jerked his pleasure into Danni's mouth, her lower extremities jerking into Sophia's. The hosts knew that their guests had been sufficiently taken care of, and it was time for them to bring themselves to a close so that they could get on with what they had invited Stephen and Danni for.

Paul thrust steadily into Danni, pacing himself just enough so that the pleasure was hers until his eruption. As he spilled over into Danni again, he brought Sophia to her own end, Sophia's mouth, her tongue especially, still on Danni.

"That was certainly interesting," Paul said as he helped Sophia to her feet.

"It was incredible. Thank you very much..." Stephen said, not sure if he should shake his hand.

Instead, he helped Danni up, and they were shown where they could shower. In the cubicle, the water was warm falling all over them, they didn't speak. They just kissed and touched a lot. Stephen was hard again, and Danni was glad. She did do this to her husband, and she liked the fact that she wielded such power. Stephen also held incredible power over her, because she was also yearning for him now, desperately wanting him inside her.

They started to make love, again no games. The

passionate exchange of their bodies was beautiful to watch if they'd had an audience. But it was just the two of them, more in love with each other even though they had just shared themselves with others. This sharing made them realize that they were open to much more than they had thought. They both wondered, without saying anything, whether they would do this again, and with whom?

These questions lingered as they made love for the longest time, really enjoying each other!

"What are your plans for the rest of your trip?" Paul asked as they sat down to dinner.

"We really have no plans. We just want to enjoy Paris and each other..." Stephen said, looking at Danni with love.

It was obvious that they really loved each other, as obvious as was Paul's love for Sophia. The four of them, enjoying the *coq au vin*, wondered if they would do this again, with each other. They had all, in their individual capacity and as a unit, enjoyed it. But nobody asked, something about the completeness of this experience making them all feel that it really wasn't the time to broach this possibility.

Paul did ask, rather cheekily, where Danni's panties were. They all laughed, Danni responding that she'd leave that for Sophia and him to discover.

Stephen was looking at Sophia again. But it wasn't lust on his face now. It was more curiosity. He looked like he wanted to ask her something, but wasn't sure how. He thought of all the reasons why this question might not sit well with his wife or her husband.

He looked at Paul, wondering if he shouldn't perhaps ask him. After all, chances were he bought it for her anyway. But before he could bring out the words in a sentence, Danni asked Sophia, "You've got to give me the name of your perfume..."

Paul got up to get another bottle of wine as the three of them laughed at the joke that nobody knew was even a joke. Stephen looked at his wife and shook his head, wondering how he had gotten so damn lucky!

ABOUT THE AUTHOR

Tena Seldan is an emerging erotica author of many erotica kinks and sub-genres. Be sure to check out other books and leave a review if this story got you hot!

Visit my blog at Tena Seldan Blog

Join my newsletter for exclusive previews

Tena Seldan Newsletter

Sign up for Free Stories from Xplicit Press Authors

Xplicit Press Author Updates

Like Xplicit Press on Facebook

Follow Xplicit Press on Twitter

Readers: I want to expand a few of the stories to see where the characters can be explored further. If there are any of the stories that you would like to read more about again, I'd love to hear from you!

Keep In Touch
Tena Seldan
info@tenaseldan.com